THE CROSS RABBIT

NICK BUTTERWORTH

Collins

An Imprint of HarperCollins*Publishers*

It was a bright, cold winter's day. Snow had fallen in the night and now everything in the park had been turned into a guessing game.

"It looks wonderful," said Percy the park keeper, "but it makes a lot of work."

Standing next to Percy was a rather old and cross looking rabbit.

"Well, quite so," said the rabbit. "But now, what about these mice? They're making a dreadful nuisance of themselves."

Percy found it hard not to laugh when he saw what was making the rabbit so cross.

The mice were having great fun.

Percy began to chuckle, but quickly turned the chuckle into a cough. After all, this was no fun for an old rabbit who only wanted to curl up and sleep through the cold weather.

"Now come along, you mice," said Percy. "You must go and play somewhere else. And," he added, "try to stay out of mischief."

The mice looked very disappointed. Slowly they walked away, dragging their toboggans behind them.

The old rabbit said thank you to Percy and then disappeared into his burrow.

Percy got on with clearing the snow. It was hot work even in the cold weather. First he took off his cap. Then his scarf. And then, even his gloves.

Percy worked hard all morning.
He mopped his brow again and
looked at his work.

"Very good," he said to himself.
"I think I deserve a spot of lunch."

Percy reached for his bag and pulled out a flask.

"That's funny," he said. "I'm sure I put the cup on the top this morning."

"I know, I'll have my yogurt first and drink from the empty carton."

Percy took out a strawberry yogurt and began to rummage through his bag. "That's odd," he said. "No spoon. Hmm."

It was a strange lunch. A lid was missing from a small box of dates and the bottom half of one of Percy's cheese rolls had disappeared. And Percy was sure he had packed an orange but there was no sign of it now. It was all very puzzling.

It felt colder to Percy as he went back to
work. He reached for his scarf and his
cap, but now they had disappeared too!

" This is most peculiar," said Percy. Then, as he gazed around looking for his cap and scarf, Percy was amazed to see his gloves walking off by themselves!

"I must be dreaming," said Percy.

"I'd like to be dreaming," said a cross voice. It was the old rabbit again.
"Those mice are making a terrible noise. Would you speak to them please?" And with that the rabbit stumped off.

Percy followed.

"Look!" said the rabbit.
Percy looked. The mice had been very busy indeed! And they were having a marvellous time.

"Hello Percy!" they called. But suddenly they looked worried. "You're not going to tell us to stop, are you?"

Percy glanced at the old rabbit.

"Well. . .no," he said to the mice. "We just wondered if you could have a marvellous time a little more quietly?"

The mice cheered.

"We'll try!" they squeaked loudly.

"Come on," said Percy to the rabbit. "I think I've got some cotton wool in my bag. A little in each ear should do the trick."

NICK BUTTERWORTH

Nick Butterworth was born in North
London in 1946 and grew up in a sweet-
shop in Essex. He now lives in Suffolk with
his wife Annette and their two children,
Ben and Amanda.

The inspiration for the Percy's
Park books came from Nick's
many walks through the local
park with the family dog, Jake. *One Snowy Night,*
the first story about Percy the park keeper and
his animal friends, was published in 1989 and
was an instant success. Now stories about
Percy and his friends are firm favourites with
children everywhere.